Nobody Knew What To Do
A STORY ABOUT BULLYING

WRITTEN BY Becky Ray McCain

ILLUSTRATED BY Todd Leonardo

ALBERT WHITMAN & COMPANY

MORTON GROVE, ILLINOIS

Library of Congress Cataloging-in-Publication Data

McCain, Becky R. (Becky Ray)

Nobody knew what to do : a story about bullying /

by Becky Ray McCain; illustrated by Todd Leonardo.

p. cm.

Summary: When bullies pick on a boy at school,

a classmate is afraid, but decides that he must do something.

ISBN 0-8075-5711-0

[1. Bullies — Fiction. 2. Schools — Fiction.]   I. Leonardo, Todd, ill. II. Title.

PZ7.M122842 No 2001   [E] — dc21   00-010520

Published in 2001 by Albert Whitman & Company,

6340 Oakton Street, Morton Grove, Illinois 60053-2723.

Published simultaneously in Canada by General Publishing, Limited, Toronto.

The illustrations were done in oil on primed paper.

The text type is Cronos.

The design is by Scott Piehl.

Nobody likes to think about it,
even though we know
it is not okay
to hurt a person
with words, or things,
or with the way we behave.

So when some kids in my class
started picking on Ray
when the teachers were busy and just couldn't see,
nobody knew what to do.

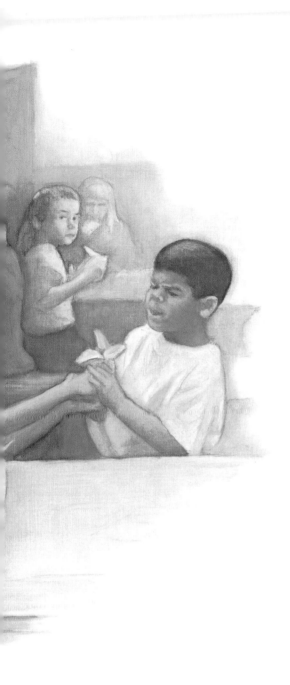

I could not find a way
to tell them to stop,
so I squeezed my eyes shut,
closed my mouth very tight,
cupped my hands to my ears,
and hoped the mean words
would fade away.

Ray was trying
hard to be brave.
I hoped he could keep going
until he fit in.

The next recess, we bunched together.
Nobody said,
"I feel safer this way."
We just did.

Except Ray.

The bullies yanked him
out of our group.
They used words and fists
to make us all so afraid,
that nobody, not one of us,
would *ever* say,
"This is NOT okay."

Next morning, Ray didn't come to school.

At recess, the ones who bullied
started cheering
because Ray wasn't around.
I didn't mean to,
but I heard bad things
they were planning to do
when Ray came back to school.

That's when I knew I had to do something.
I walked quietly to my teacher,
because she listens.

I told her what had happened to Ray.
She said I helped
by telling the truth,
so we could all figure out what to do.

When Ray came back,
he looked nervous and afraid.
So I said, "Play with us at recess."
And he did.
You know what?
When the kids who bullied
came around…

so did my teacher.
So did my principal.

And she called
the parents of everyone
who had been mean to Ray.

Nobody bullied that day.
We won't let it happen.

Together we know what to do
and say
to make sure bullying is NEVER okay.
We work together to make it end.

A Note About Bully Prevention

The day when children were advised to "fight back" to stop bullying is fast ending. As we continue to address bullying, we are learning to sort reality from myth and determine what does and does not work. "Kids will be kids" is less frequently heard among adults as an explanation for physical and verbal bullying.

Instead, we are finding that this challenge is best met when we pull together. We can teach our children there are better choices to use in potentially hurtful and violent situations. These techniques help prevent bullying, and a few are listed here:

- Let children know that it is *okay* to walk away from a fight and find grownup help instead.

- When a child is being verbally bullied, he should be encouraged to take a few seconds to think before responding. Just taking a breath instead of speaking back in anger can help defuse a volatile situation, and it's important for children to recognize that this is a commendable choice — not a weak one.

- While "tattling" just spreads stories that don't help, *telling* lets adults know what happened in a bullying situation and enables them to address the problem. Children sometimes have trouble understanding this distinction, so they need reminders that it is *always* okay to talk to parents, teachers, and other familiar grownups.

When bullying happens, people are often scared and don't know what to do. At these times, a child might think bullying is an accepted behavior. However, when children learn and use bully prevention techniques and see them used by others as well, their confidence against bullies increases. Children can learn that nonviolent bully prevention techniques work, particularly when they are used in a school setting with adult encouragement and support.

Finally, adopting a schoolwide NO TOLERANCE policy toward bullying can provide all members of the school community — teachers, parents and caregivers, and students — a foundation for teaching and encouraging positive practices. There are a growing number of programs and curricula sources that can be used to teach schools nonviolent techniques to replace bullying.

Bully prevention techniques are essential, and, like other skills in school, they must be taught, rehearsed, and refined until everyone knows what to do.

—Becky Ray McCain

For Emma and Don.
With special thanks to the students and staff
of Village East Elementary School.
— B. R. M.

For Nicholas.
With special thanks to Ms. Rider and
her students at Chabot School.
— T. L.